AN ELECTRIC SECRET

Adapted by Maria S. Barbo

©2023 Pokémon. ©1997–2020 Nintendo, Creatures, GAME FREAK,
TV Tokyo, ShoPro, JR Kikaku. TM, ® Nintendo.

ISBN 978-1-338-87140-1

10 9 8 7 6 5 4 3 2   23 24 25 26 27

Printed in the U.S.A.   40

First printing 2023

Designed by Cheung Tai

SCHOLASTIC INC.

Ash's Pikachu stood in a lineup with other Electric-type Pokémon.

Someone was stealing electricity from homes in town!

Detective Decker had a drawing of the thief.

"It's you!" he shouted. He pointed at Pikachu.
"Spill the beans!"

Pikachu was confused.

"This is messed up!" said Ash. "Pikachu hasn't done anything wrong!"

The detective put handcuffs on the little Pokémon.

They were too big.

"Pika! Pika pika!"
Pikachu shouted. It
could sense the thief
striking again!

It dashed down the
street to a house.

A man ran out of the house screaming, "A thief stole my electricity!"

"Curses!" Detective Decker cried.

"This is good news!" said Officer Jenny. "Now we know Pikachu can help us catch the REAL thief!"

"We want to help, too!" said Ash and Goh.
Officer Jenny gave them uniforms to wear.
They were going to be police officers for the day!

Ash and Goh wanted to catch the electricity thief.

But there were so many other Pokémon and Trainers who needed help, too!

First, they helped a boy find his Vulpix in a park FULL of Vulpix.

Its tail was shaped like a heart, but it was still really hard to find.

Then Ash and Goh shoved a snoozing Snorlax off the street.

They chased a dashing Dodrio.

They helped a group of Psyduck cross the road and untangled two Tangela.

"I had no idea Officer Jenny was so busy!" said Ash.

The friends were tired. But they still had not found the thief!

"We need a plan," said Ash.

Pikachu's cheeks sparked.

"I've got it!" said Goh. "If Pikachu fills a house with a lot of electricity, the thief will come to us!"

They raced to their friend's house.
Pikachu used Thunderbolt to blast the
house with electricity.

"Pika-chuuuuuuuu!" Pikachu shouted.

"Now what?" asked Goh.

"Now we wait," said Ash.

Goh pulled out the drawing of the thief.

A Pikachu could blast energy. But it could not drain energy.

Which Pokémon could? A Dedenne? Or some other kind of Pokémon?

"A Morpeko!" Ash cried.

Eevee and Yamper had cornered a Morpeko under the kitchen table. It was eating stolen food.

"But Morpeko can't drain electricity either," said Ash.

The Pokémon ran out of the house, and Ash followed it.

"Aha! TEAM ROCKET!" Ash shouted.

Jessie, James, and Meowth were using a giant machine to suck all the energy out of the house! They thought it would feed their Morpeko.

"You're under arrest for grand theft of electricity!" said Officer Jenny.

"No chain is gonna cuff me!" Jessie said.

"Later!" James called.

Team Rocket hopped in their car and sped away.
The heroes raced after them.

"Now, Growlithe!" called Officer Jenny. "Swift, let's go!"
Growlithe tried to knock Team Rocket off the road.

But Meowth launched an electrical
boom at the patrol car.
"Boo-ya!" he shouted.

The patrol car spun out.
"They're eating our dust," said Meowth.
"No muss, no fuss," said James.

The electricity thieves had gotten away again!

Soon the patrol car screeched to a stop inside Team Rocket's hideout. "Pikachu, use Thunderbolt. It's double payback time!" Ash said.

Pikachu used the stolen electricity to build up an extra-large attack. "PIKAAAAA!"

It hit Team Rocket. "We're blasting off again!" they wailed.

Back in Cerise Park, Detective Decker gave Pikachu an award.

"Thanks for a job well done, Pikachu," he said. "We'll call you Detective PIKA-PIKA-PIKA-PIKA-PIKA power!"